PUCKSTER PLAYS
THE HOCKEY MASCOTS

CANADA

FENN
TUNDRA

BY LORNA SCHULTZ NICHOLSON
ILLUSTRATED BY KELLY FINDLEY

Puckster and his pals were getting ready to play the Mascots. Some were even from the NHL. Carlton the Bear was the mascot for the Toronto Maple Leafs, and Puckster had his autograph hanging on his wall. Youppi was from the Montreal Canadiens. He'd been a mascot for two professional sport teams—the Canadiens and the Montreal Expos baseball team! Puckster didn't know any animal who had done *that* before.

"Aren't you nervous?" Charlie asked Puckster.

"My tummy is in knots." Puckster put his hand on his stomach.

"You'll do great!" Charlie reached up and patted Puckster on the back. Usually it was Puckster who encouraged Charlie, but today it was the other way around.

"Thanks, Charlie," he said. He took a deep breath to calm his nerves.

A few minutes later, Puckster stepped on the ice. He was so nervous that his legs wobbled.

"Just treat it like any other game," whispered Sarah as she skated past.

"Thanks," said Puckster. All of his pals were being so nice.

Puckster lined up at the faceoff against Carlton. He was a big bear, and strong. Puckster stared at the puck. When it dropped he fought hard and won the battle. He fired it over to Francois on the wing. Puckster flew up the ice.

"Francois," he called out. "I'm open!"

Francois passed him the puck and Puckster skated hard toward the Mascots goalie. As he wheeled down the ice, he heard Charlie yelling that he was open. But Puckster kept the puck on his stick. If he could score, his heroes would all think he was a good player! Puckster made another deke and fired off a hard wrist shot. It sank to the back of the net.

Puckster raised his hands in the air as his teammates rushed over.

"Good work, Puckster," said Manny.

As Puckster glided to the bench, Carlton skated past. "Nice goal," he said.

Puckster beamed.

Puckster skated as fast as he could on every shift. Near the end of the period, Puckster once again had the puck. This time, it was Francois who yelled out, "I'm open!"

But Puckster ignored him. He wanted another goal.

He wound up and blasted a shot. The puck hit the goalie's mask and bounced into the back of the net.

"You're on fire today," said Sarah, patting his back.

"It's great you scored, but I was open," said Francois.

As Puckster made his way to the bench, Youppi skated past. "You have an amazing shot," he said.

Puckster grinned. If he scored one more he'd have a hat trick! Then they'd think he was a real star.

"We're doing great," Puckster said to his teammates on the bench. He slurped down some water and wiped his mouth.

"You're doing great," said Francois. He turned his back to Puckster.

"Yeah. None of us have even touched the puck," moped Charlie. "When we practise, you always tell us to pass the puck. Now you're just hogging it."

"No, I'm not," said Puckster, frowning. "I just want us to win."

He looked at all his pals. "Don't you guys want to win?"

The buzzer sounded to start the second period. Puckster quickly skated to the faceoff circle. He had a plan. When the puck dropped, instead of sending it over to Francois or Charlie on the wings, he smacked it forward and skated around Carlton. When he got the puck on the end of his stick, he raced toward the goalie. But Youppi swung in and stole the puck.

The Mascots raced toward Roly. Puckster screeched to a stop, turned, and gave chase, but he couldn't catch them. Youppi passed to Carlton. Carlton passed back to Youppi. Youppi passed back to Carlton. Carlton wound up for a slap shot and sent it sailing past Roly.

Puckster gritted his teeth. He needed to get another goal. And fast.

For the rest of the period, Puckster skated and skated, up and down the ice. He tried as hard as he could to score. He deked and took wrist shots and snap shots and slap shots.

But the puck just wouldn't go in the net. One more goal. He needed just one more to get that hat trick. Sweat dripped from his forehead.

With one minute left in the period, Youppi stole the puck from Puckster *again* and skated down the ice. Puckster was so tired. Youppi passed to Carlton. Carlton passed to a Mascot teammate on the opposite wing. All the way down the ice they passed the puck, like they were playing ping-pong. When Youppi sniped off a wrist shot, Roly didn't have a chance.

The buzzer went. It was now a tie game after two periods. Puckster hung his head as he skated to the bench.

"We're not going to win," said Charlie as he gulped down water.

"That's not a very good attitude," replied Puckster.

"But he's right," said Sarah. "We aren't playing like a team."

"Yeah, we're playing like individuals," said Manny.

"Especially you, Puckster," said Charlie. "I was open at least ten times."

"Don't you like playing with us anymore?" Francois asked quietly.

Puckster stared at his pals. They all looked so sad! Puckster's shoulders slumped. He reached out his hand so it was in the middle of the group. "Let's cheer," he said.

Slowly, everyone put their hands on top of Puckster's, but when they cheered it sounded more like a low moan.

The Mascots blasted out for the third period. Puckster lined up at the faceoff circle. When he won the draw, he sent the puck back to Manny. Manny fired it to Sarah, who passed it to Charlie. Puckster skated forward. When he got near the net he called out to Charlie.

Charlie looked up and batted the puck to him. Out of the corner of his eye, Puckster saw Francois at the side of the net.

Puckster thought he could probably score—and get that hat trick—but Francois had a way better chance. He faked a shot then passed the puck.

Francois nailed a shot into the back of the net.

Francois jumped up and down. Puckster grinned and high-fived his teammate.

"Wow," said Youppi and Carlton. "Now *that* was a great play."

Puckster smiled his biggest smile of the game.

21 🍁

The Mascots scored one more goal and the game ended in a tie. Both teams lined up to shake hands.

Puckster let his friends go first. And when it was his turn, he got Youppi's autograph. It would look great on his wall, right next to Carlton's!

PUCKSTER'S TIPS:

If you play on a team, all of your teammates are important.

Encourage your friends to be the best they can be.

Getting an assist is as important as getting a goal.

PUCKSTER'S HOCKEY TIP:

A **hat trick** is when one player on a team scores **three** goals.

Good luck!